Nightie Night, Lucy!

Story and
illustrations
by Sally O. Lee

I would like to thank Stephanie Robinson, Sarah Lange Davis
and the staff at BookSurge for their encouragement in helping
me to write and illustrate this book.

www.booksurge.com

Also, I would like to thank my family and friends
for their love and support.

This book is typeset in Garamond.

www.leepublishing.net

To: Mumzy

who has always supported me
as an artist, and who provided
me with copious amounts of
art supplies as a kid.
Thank you for everything.
I love you.

Lucy's mother exclaimed.

t was time for bed.
But, as you know,
Lucy was not ready
to go to sleep.....

and neither was Seymour.

So, first they
decided to fly
through space.

Then, Lucy became
a ballerina on a
big stage
with bright lights.

Seymour rode his motorcycle through the rolling, green mountains.

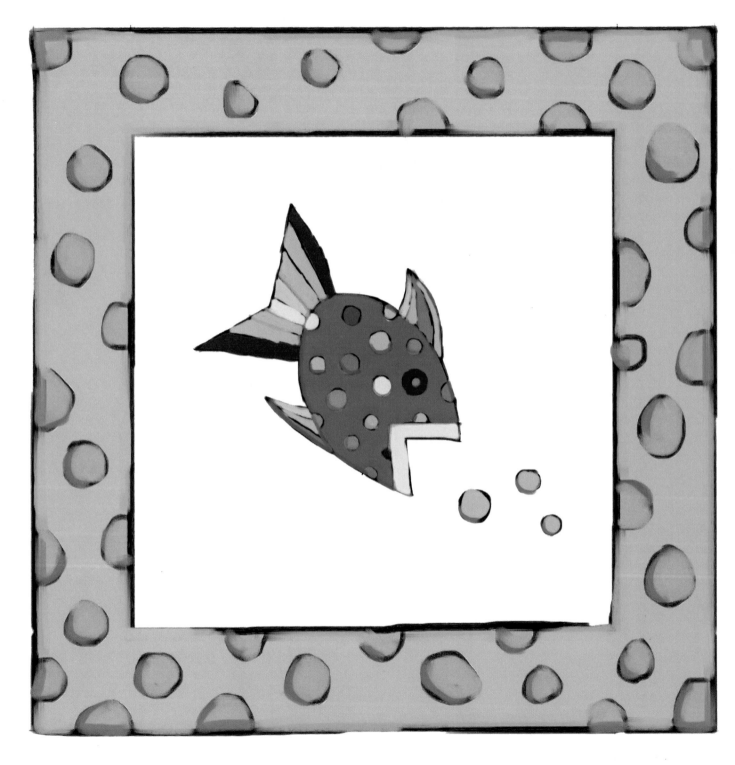

Lucy and Seymour
dove into
the waters
of the deep ocean
and swam with
all the colorful fish.

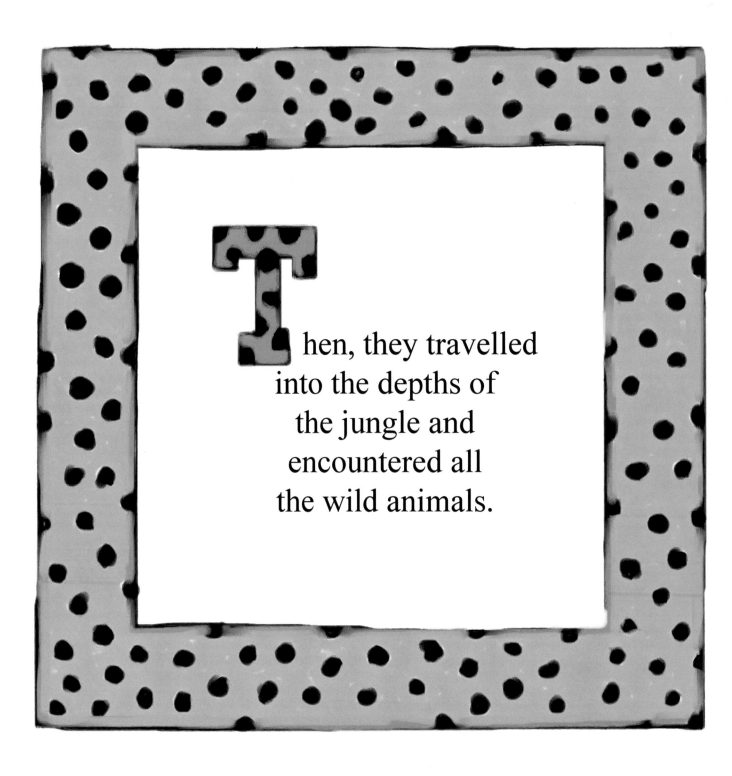

Then, they travelled into the depths of the jungle and encountered all the wild animals.

ut now it was really time
for Lucy to go to bed,
so her mother said,
"Nightie, Night, Lucy."

And Lucy said,
"Nightie Night, Mumzy."
and fell
fast asleep.